ALL ABOARD READING™

PICTURE READER

IN A DARK, DARK HOUSE

P9-CEC-744

By Jennifer Dussling
Illustrated by Davy Jones

Grosset & Dunlap • New York

The ☀ went down.

The ✦ came out.

The 🕙 struck ten.

And I went walking

under a dark,

dark 🌙.

And under that dark,

dark ,

I saw a dark,

dark .

Was I scared?

NO!

And past that dark,

dark ,

I saw a dark,

dark .

I went in the .

Was I scared?

NO!

And in the dark,

dark  ,

I went up some dark,

dark  .

Was I scared?

NO!

And at the end

of the dark,

dark ,

I saw a dark,

dark .

I opened the .

Was I scared?

NO!

And behind the dark,

dark ,

I found a dark,

dark .

Was I scared?

NO!

I opened the dark,

dark .

And inside

was a—

MONSTER!

It had three !

A green !

Long

and sharp !

Was I scared?

YES!

I shut the .

I slammed the .

I ran down the

and out of the .

I ran and ran—

past the .

No! Not past the .

Up the !

Safe at last,

under the dark,

dark .

door	clock
chest	moon
house	nose

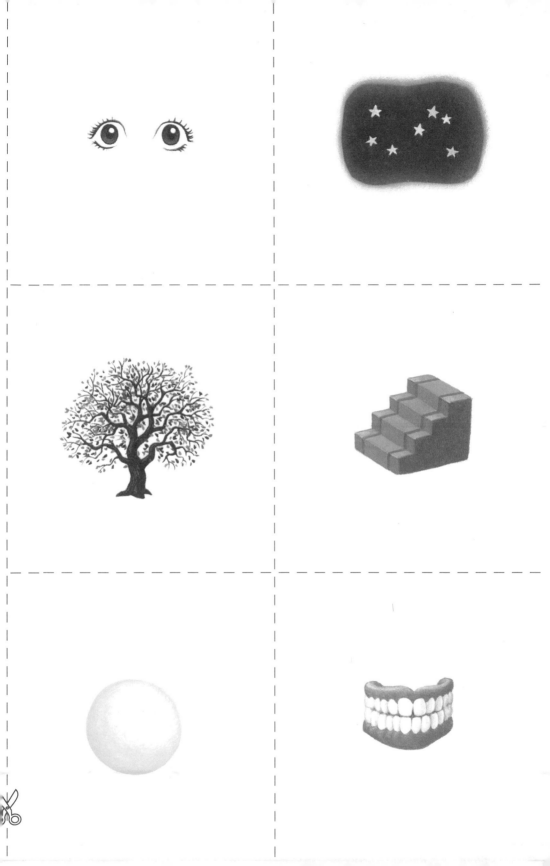

stars	eyes
stairs	tree
teeth	sun

book	claws
duck	ball
cat	truck

bed	apple
bus	dog
bike	cake